Peter Gimpel

PROFESSOR GANSA'S DREAM

or

Science as a Naked Lightbulb

a
Parable
in 75 "Stanzos"
comprising

a
Jewish
reply to
Carl Sagan's

The Demon-Haunted World:
Science as a Candle in the Dark

Red Heifer Press

PROFESSOR

GANSA'S

DREAM

PROFESSOR GANSA'S DREAM, or . . .
Science as a Naked Lightbulb: a Jewish reply to Carl Sagan's
The Demon-Haunted World: Science as a Candle in the Dark.
Copyright © 2003 by Peter Gimpel
First Edition
Published in the United States by Red Heifer Press,
P.O. Box 1891, Beverly Hills, California 90213-1891.
All rights reserved.

With eleven Visualizations by Gerry McGuinness.
Cover art by Gerry McGuinness.
Cover design by Jorge A. Pringles (L.A. Press)
Typesetting and book design by Red Heifer Press.

Library of Congress Control Number: 2002 190011
ISBN: 0-9631478-3-8

A NOTE TO THE READER

The figure of Carlo Gansa is a fictional reconstruction, based almost exclusively on the contents of Carl Sagan's book, *The Demon-Haunted World: Science as a Candle in the Dark,* as interpreted by my imagination under the direction of reasonable inference. As a critic of his book, I would prefer that Carl Sagan were still alive. However, the awesomeness of books in general is that the limited immortality they confer upon their authors is tied to an undying responsibility for what they have written.

—Peter Gimpel

For Audrey, my Patient Muse

Dim, as the borrow'd beams of Moon and Stars
To *lonely, weary, wandring* Travellers
Is *Reason* to the *Soul:* And as on high,
Those rowling Fires *discover* but the Sky
Not light as *here;* So *Reason's* glimmering Ray
Was lent, not to *assure* our *doubtfull* way,
But *guide* us upward to a *better* Day.
And as those nightly Tapers disappear
When Day's bright Lord ascends our Hemisphere;
So Pale grows *Reason* at *Religions* Sight;
So *dies,* and so *dissolves* in *Supernatural Light.*

—Dryden

"Reason's Glimmering Ray"

Call you 'em stanzos?
                    —*As you Like it*

PROFESSOR GANSA'S DREAM

or

SCIENCE AS A NAKED LIGHTBULB

I

Minus his labcoat, clad in Gucci suit,
or casually attired in cashmere cardigan,
his choice of necktie cunningly astute,
he cut a stylish figure; but *en retard* again,
still smocked in white, Professor Carlo Gansa
looked more the ghost than priest of *eleganza*
(but who am I to talk—a shrink playing bard again?)
as he rushed to lock the doors and drawers of his inner sanctum—
his private labs and the offices which flanked 'em.

II

He had been working late. His staff, long gone,
conspirators bound in innocent conspiracy,
had left him and his white lab rats alone,
to plot the final touches to their heresy—
a party with his publisher, to crook
an elbow with their boss at his new book,
a bash with E and M enough to square a C—
all unbeknownst, of course, to the benign professor—
as they used to say, "not even his hairdresser . . ."!

III

Gansa did not believe in ghosts or priests,
for all he may have looked like one or the other.
His book deplored the mass mystique that feasts
on ignorance, the latter being the mother
of tyranny, religion, plague and slaughter—
fey superstition being the eldest daughter—
although one had to wonder if the author
completely grasped the finer points and deeper reasons
for the alternation of the human seasons.

IV

Some saw him as a labcoat Don Quixote,
tilting at windmills—UFO's, the Bible,
the ban on marijuana and peyote,
and other follies to which the race is liable—
mind-readers, homeopaths, faces on Mars,
and alien abductions (with genital scars!);
witch-burnings and necromancy, *que diable!*
But science education was his Dulcinea,
and, for the nation's woes, his panacea.

V

His book had made the *New York Times* bestseller list,
and several of the critics waxed ecstatic.
But Gansa had not made all folks' good-feller list.
The reception had not been without some static.
Indeed, some said he singled out the Jews
for special criticism and abuse,
portraying them as fundamentalist, fanatic,
and, *note well* (this takes the cake!): historically cruel,
thus feeding the fires of hate with yet more fuel.

IV: UFOs, the Bible, etc. For background on this agenda, see Note 1 at end.

V: Special criticism and abuse, etc.: See Note 2 at end.

Faces on Mars

VI

Outraged, some branded him an antisemite.
"How can a Semite be antisemitic?"
he would reply. "I am a Jew, a Semite!
My objections are religious, not genetic!"
Yet in regard to Haman and Amalek,
what gave Professor Gansa such a colic
(although his tone remained purely noetic!)
was that the Jews did not with due cooperation
fully comply in their own annihilation!

VII

The proof of their barbarity, he claimed,
lay in the Books of Esther and of "Saul"—
the latter book erroneously named,
proving, if anything was proved at all,
that even a fount of wisdom should never spout
on matters which it knows nothing about!
As if that weren't enough, he had the gall,
the nerve, to take his proof-text from the very Bible,
he elsewhere argues, is so unreliable!

VIII

But Gansa, in my professional opinion,
was neither antisemite nor agnostic:
though doubting G–d and consequence to sin yon,
he kept for his own kindred his most caustic
barbs, shot sea-to-shore with special rancor
at those he spied with envy safe at anchor.
Rank envy was the crux and the acrostic
of all he said against his own religion's name,
and it upset his judgement and his aim.

VI: Haman and Amalek: See Note 3 at end.

IX

But I don't mean to run on to excess.
His bag, though mixed, was not devoid of merit.
Besides, his book was clearly a success.
It was time to party, or time to grin and bear it.
We left the venerable man of knowledge
preparing to depart campus and college—
a good man with a heart of fourteen karat,
good husband and good dad, devoted to his students,
and stable of laboratory rodents.

X

(What intercourse a mouse has with astronomy,
I failed to ask, and thus I cannot say.
He was such a polymath, it didn't dawn on me
till later that the stars were his mainstay.)
As I was saying some nine-or-so lines backing up,
we left our latter-day La Mancha packing up.
He bid his favorite labmouse, Stephen Jay,
an affectionate farewell and a serene goodnight,
and setting the alarm, turned off the light.

XI

A mild September evening, and the stars
shone on the parking lot in mute apology
as Gansa groped through parking pocked like Mars,
occasionally uttering a scatology.
They seemed to clamor in their gleaming hoards
like stars at an Academy Awards,
winking as if they knew from their astrology
that what was about to happen would be scarcely credible
to the editor of *Tales of the Incredible!*

XII

Of course, his scopes would not be aimed at stars
while navigating through the potholed parking lot:
earthward he pivoted his Palomars,
oblivious of the whole resplendent, arcing lot.
What's more, the pupils of our Galilei
were not what once they were in their heyday,
and like a cat pursued by a wild, barking lot,
Professor Gansa's eyes, emergent from his lair,
were wide with fear, and nightblind from the glare.

XIII

He was to have met his wife at the hotel
(it was the posh and elegant Pendragon)
She'd told him what they'd planned for her to tell.
The two of them would party with a flagon.
She'd bring his toothbrush, slippers and pajamas—
they'd fantasize a night in the Bahamas . . .
But Gansa never made it to his wagon.
He awoke in hospital, hooked up and gowned, in bed,
with a bandage round his ankle and his head.

XIV

According to what Gansa told me later,
it took some months until his shattered memory
revived. Till then, he felt like an ice-skater
caught in a kind of ominous ice-mummery
upon thin ice stretched over a deep abyss,
cutting weird figures with a ghastly hiss.
To make it short and put it all in summary,
his mind began to crack together with the ice.
That's when he sought my medical advice.

XV

When Gansa showed up in my office, he,
though smockless, nonetheless looked like a ghost—
and certainly not the man seen on T.V.
promoting science to a talk-show host.
Discreetly sitting down behind the fern,
he started by expressing great concern
lest matters become known from coast to coast.
I cited him our ethics code, chapter and verse,
and hid my poems, not to make matters worse.

XVI

He commenced his story about where I left off—
in the parking lot, between crater and boulder,
when suddenly, behind his back, a cough!—
and someone taps him smartly on the shoulder.
"I sprinted to my car, and tore my pocket
trying to extract my car keys to unlock it.
As I fumbled with the keys, the air grew colder.
I swivelled 'round and saw the shadow of the being
whose icy hand prevented me from fleeing.

XVII

"What I am trying to say is that the hand
pursued me as I ran—the being stayed put.
As in a child's bad dream, I lost command
of limb, like Gulliver in Lilliput."
I asked, could he describe the thing, the being?
"Words can't give shape to what my eyes were seeing,
but it looked like something out of east *Galut*—
a Jew with beard and sidelocks, *talis* and *tefilin* . . .
I leave the rest to you, Doctor, to fill in!"

XVII: *Galut:* The Exile, or Diaspora. East *Galut:* Eastern Europe.
          Talis: Prayer shawl.
          Tefellin: The Phylacteries.

...and hid my poems, not to make matters worse.

XVIII

"Did it have a hat—one of those weird fur hats?"
I asked. "Oh yes! I think they call them 'strudel.' "
"That's *Streumel,*" I corrected. "Well then, that's
what that looked like. The whole kit and kaboodle—
a strudelled rabbi—Something -stein or -steen—
as I was to learn, of late from Golders Green.
I stared at him and shook like a toy poodle."
Here, I confess, I coughed and gave a squirm and wiggle,
trying mightily to cover up a giggle.

XIX

"You smirk, Sir! Don't suppress a laugh for my sake!
You think I'm pusilanimous—admit it!
But for all I knew, this was the work of Isaac—
that's Asimov—whom I had often twitted . . . !
The thing just stood there pointing with its arm
above my head. 'This means the funny farm,'
I thought. 'I'll have to have myself comitted!'
For, hovering at roof height like some enormous saucer,
was something out of *Bluebook's* secret dossier.

XX

"I see, Sir, that you've heard the lurid details
of tractor beams and rays and ramps of light
that suck you helpless into the entrails
of alien ships straight from your bed at night;
and all my life I thought that I would welcome
the chance to board a UFO, come hell, come
high water, and would have now, if not for fright.
As it was, I ascended by dilapidated ladder—
and ascended fast, owing to an aching bladder.

XIX: Bluebook's *secret dossier:* "Project Bluebook" was the U.S. Air
Force's early and much-criticized study of UFO sightings.

XXI

" 'At least, a UFO should have facilities!'
I thought, but once inside, I lost the urge
in my desire to explore their capabilities;
and when a dozen of these beings emerge,
my first words are, 'Please show me your technology!'
Their leader smiles, 'Technology, schmecknology!
You come with us.' At once, they all converge.
'Drink this, *Shaygetz!*' says one, proffering me a dram,
'we'll do a schmecknological exam.'

XXII

"They led me to the examination room
by what seemed like a complicated route.
I could not see much through the twilit gloom.
I longed for light, but they could see without,
and, after a while, it seems I, too, was able.
They laid me flat, then, on a wooden table.
The last thing I recall before passing out
were the straps that held me down being tightened up a notch,
and one of them's hands busy at my crotch.

XXIII

"I woke up looking at an azure sky
through a filigree of branches, twigs and leaves.
I lay, as I discovered by and by,
upon a bed of moss like Adam-and-Eve's,
when G–d created them by blowing His breath
in them, conferring on them life and death.
I was as one who, doubting long, believes
at last—or rather learns and knows and understands—
and I grabbed this as a gift with both my hands.

XXI: Shaygetz: "Non-Jew"; applied disparagingly to a Jew who knows and
cares nothing about Judaism or his Jewish heritage.

"The thing just stood there pointing with its arm…"

XXIV

"Turning my head, I saw a distant plain
pursuing an infinitely fleeing horizon.
My sight joined the pursuit, pursuing in vain,
for I encountered naught to fix my eyes on,
except such obstacles as checked their course—
great mountains, sculpted with titanic force,
snowpeaks such as the sun blissfully dies on,
broad rivers wriggling like gigantic, silver snakes,
forests and fields and hills and deep-blue lakes . . .

XXV

"I saw that I lay upon a rugged ridge
that jutted over catastrophic canyons,
my pinnacle conjoined by a soaring bridge
to towering coryphees, distant companions
in the diamantine air, whence issued strains
of purest music with sublime refrains,
which seemed to come from structures shaped like onions
clinging in clusters round the tops of their lookouts,
and looking like tremendous Brussels sprouts.

XXVI

This was the music of concerted prayers,
collected from *Minyanim* the world over,
and sung to the instruments of Levite players
in harmonies the great composers strove for,
to a counterpoint of little children's voices
reciting Torah, in which the L–rd rejoices.
I was certain, in such a garden, to discover
a chorus of *Kiddushas* and amens to *Kaddish*
housed in a golden dome shaped like a radish!

———————————————————

XXVI: *Minyanim:* Prayer congregations.

    Kiddushas (pl.): The *Kiddusha* is a segment of the morning and
afternoon prayers, recited responsively and in unison.

(Note continues next page . . .)

XXVII

"The view was like (if I'm not being too gauche,
and if the example isn't too abstruse)
a triptych by the Flemish painter Bosch—
collaborated on by Doctor Seuss!
My company upon my exalted perch
was nothing but a large stone and a birch—
both smooth and white and of no likely use
in terms of finding my way back to the spaceship,
or attaining the objectives of my trip.

XXVIII

"Oddly enough, I felt no fear or dread
on seeing myself in such a tight predicament,
but gamely leapt up from my mossy bed
on discovering myself bound by no ligament.
Blithe spirit! For suddenly the stone began
to move, stood up and stretched, became a man,
and smoothed the regal folds of his integument.
It was none other than that Mr. -stein, or -steen,
whose prisoner, not long ago, I'd been.

XXIX

"Seeing him in broad daylight, I saw the truth.
In spite of me, I blurted, 'You're a Jew!'
though I confess, it *was* rather uncouth.
But he just looked me over coolly. *'Nu?'*
was all he said. He pointed to a pool
of crystal water, gleaming like a jewel
set in the rock, distilled from mossy dew,
and handing me a golden washing cup, with mimes
and gestures bade me wash my hands three times.

(XXVI): Kaddish: A special prayer recited by the leader and/or a mourner, in praise of G–d, and to which the congregation must respond "amen" at specified intervals.

Ol' Pototzky's not-so-kosher deli

XXX

"Thus sanctified, I felt a timid pang
of incipient hunger stir inside my belly,
and thought how nice it would be to drive the gang
to ol' Pototzky's not-so-kosher deli
for one of 'Totzky's' hot corned beef on rye,
and thinking kind of made me want to cry—
especially when I thought of 'Totzky's' smelly
stuffed cabbages and sauerkraut washed down with beer—
and wanting to cry brought to my eye a tear.

XXXI

"In short, if I was hungry, I was starving,
and if I shed a tear, I cried a flood!
All I could think of was Pototzky carving
cold cuts on the counter beneath the hood,
and spreading mustard on a kaiser roll.
'What you need now is to restore your *soul*,'
soothed Mr. -steen. 'Look here, I brought some food!'
So saying, he fishes with a flourish of enlargement
within his robes, and extracts a scroll of parchment.

XXXII

"It looked just like one of those scrolls of Torah
you've seen being read from at a boy's Bar Mitzva
(and, so it seems, being read from till tomorrow!)—
you've seen them, too, sometimes, at a Bat Mitzva—
although I guess I shouldn't mention either,
since I myself have been called up for neither!—
except it's smaller and, more strangely, it's 'v a
piece with Mr -stein himself, parcel and part,
as if he extracted from his chest his heart!

XXXII: I myself have been called up for neither: a legitimate inference.
Compare Note 6 at end.

XXXIII

"We sat and read from the place where Abraham
prepares a feast and slaughters a young veal
to where he finds and offers up a ram;
and Mr. -stein expounded a great deal
and told me things not written in those pages—
things brought down with reverence through the ages—
secrets that I both can and can't reveal,
since part of what he told was *'nistar'*—highly classified,
and told because I begged—would not be pacified.

XXXIV

"For instance, how it was that three from heaven
could take on human form and flesh, and eat;
why the cakes that Sarah baked were without leaven;
whether the angels ate their curds with meat,
or duly waited after eating dairy;
why Abraham implored his guests to tarry,
and why he fetched them water for their feet,
and why G–d sought his help in such a grave decision
upon the third day of his circumcision.

XXXV

"And it seemed that, just as angels could partake
of earthly food and join in a repast,
so flesh and blood in the higher realms could make
a meal of what elsewhere would make a fast.
For I felt strangely, yet completely satiated
as I digested what -stein/-steen expatiated—
as though I'd just devoured a big breakfast
of bagels, lox and cream cheese, coffee, eggs and blintzes
on a kosher Caribbean cruise by Princess!

XXXIII: nistar: Literally, hidden or concealed.
XXXIV: such a grave decision: i.e., whether to destroy Sodom and
Gemorra.

"...and Mr. -stein expounded a great deal..."

XXXVI

"However, I'd still not grasped what sort of isle
I had of late been cast away or stranded on,
nor had I yet been able to reconcile
my concepts of—if I may be so candid on
so touchy a subject—UFO and Jew
(what's more, a ranking member of the crew!),
and so I asked where was the ship we'd landed on,
and how it came to pass a religious Jew should man it,
and what our purpose was upon this planet."

XXXVII

Gansa, who'd shifted from behind his potted
plant, now paused and tactfully inquired
just how much time was left of his allotted
hour. His time was up—long since expired—
but so intrigued was I by Gansa's menu,
I lied, and urged him by all means continue.
By now, I had to know all that transpired,
for many an anguished hour I'd stroked my Freudian whiskers
on that last question. But shhh! he resumed his discourse:

XXXVIII

" 'Here all is done according to the Torah.
Not one *Nekudah*'s been left out or smudged.
Do you think that you're on Mars, or Bora-Bora?
Our purpose is, you're brought here to be judged.
As for the ship,'—and here he made a minute
hand and swept around the clock—'you're in it!
This is the next world to the world you trudged.
You are not dead, but in a deep suspended state.
Your judgement will no doubt decide your fate.'

XXXVIII: Nekudah: Hebrew vowel point.

XXXIX

"Seeing that I stood there like an obelisk,
with mouth agape, hair curled in impromptu permanent,
he pointed upwards to an asterisk
suspended high in heaven's own blue firmament.
'See there,' he said. 'That is your universe!'
Somehow, it seemed a suitable reverse
that the world of passions, fleeting and impermanent,
should appear at last no bigger than a short footnote
referring to a questionable quote.

XL

"And so began a trek which by our sun
would last a year—if one could call it 'lasting'—
for it seemed to end before it was begun,
so quickly did our days and nights go blasting
through virtual space and time. I saw great wonders,
prodigious miracles, lightnings and thunders,
and characters straight out of Central Casting.
Each day we read the allotted portion of the Torah,
and studied *Tanya* and a *Blatt Gemorah*.

―――――――――――――――――

XL: Tanya: *Likutei Amarim, "Tanya"*, by Rabbi Shneur Zalman of Liadi, the fundamental Chassidic text of Chabad Chassidism.

Blatt Gemorah: A leaf of the Talmud, the daily alloted portion which learned Jews study in accordance with a universal calendar.

XLI

"And as I learned, I had the strange impression
that what I learned, I had once learned before.
I mentioned this, during one such Torah session,
to -stein. He bade me stand, and through the door
appears an angel—gorgeous, in full bloom—
the one who taught me in my mother's womb!
Remembering those idyllic days of yore,
I ran to greet him, tears of joy streaking my face,
and he wept, too, because of my disgrace.

XLII

"And so it went. We walked, we talked, we studied,
we argued over *Rambam* and *Ramchal*.
Our feet never ached, our shoes were never muddied,
although we hiked through marsh and chapparal.
We climbed over mountain passes, grassy downs,
wound up high, spiral paths to hilltop towns,
conversed with *Am ha-aretz* and *Chazal*,
with martyrs of the Holocaust and Inquisition,
and the sporadic lawyer or physician.

XLII: *Rambam:* Rabbi Moshe ben Maimon, "Maimonides", author of the *Guide of the Perplexed* and the *Mishneh Torah,* a comprehensive and monumental treatise of Jewish Law.

Ramchal: Rabbi Moshe Chaim Luzzato of Padua, author of classic works on Jewish ethics, eschatology and education.

Am ha-aretz: "People of the soil", those who have no knowledge of Torah.

Chazal: The blessed Sages of the Talmud.

XLIII

"-Steen showed me things that I could not describe
if I had a thousand tongues—all of them wagging.
I heard a cedar forest sing *'Ascribe'*
in a way that leaves imagination lagging.
I saw hills skipping, rivers running backwards,
and prodigies for which I simply lack words.
Don't think that I am dropping names or bragging
when I tell you that I met the greatest names of Israel—
saw their faces (the light from Moses' *is* real)!

XLIV

"Seeking admission to a Torah lecture
(Yehuda-ha-Nasi expounding on the Mishna
and the structure of its awesome architecture),
I was swept up by a crowd of ex-Hare-Krishna
running to hear the words of a mystery Rebbe
whose deeds were but foreshadowed by Entebbe:
a great Redeemer, King, and Requisitioner!
Rabbi Schneerson manned the entrance with a giant Hoover
that sucked up scads of souls of Baalei-Teshuva.

XLIII: Ascribe: "Ascribe invincible strength unto the Lord". *Psalms*, 68, 35.

XLIV: Yehuda-ha-Nasi: Yehuda the Prince, President of the Sanhedrin in the time of Antoninus Pius, and final editor of the fundamental compilation of Jewish law known as the *Mishna*.

Entebbe: referring to the daring and near-flawless raid (1976), in which Israeli commandos rescued over 100 skyjacked Jews held hostage at Uganda's Entebbe airport by Palestinian and German terrorists with the complicity of Idi Amin.

Baalei-Teshuva: "Masters of Repentance": Jews who return to Torah observance and to G–d.

A great Redeemer, King, and Requisitioner

XLV

"I encountered, too, the souls of righteous Goyim,
who dwell together in a crystal palace,
much frequented by Jews, who greatly enjoy 'em,
tasting each other's wine in a crystal chalice.
I visited a hospital for souls
whose forms were full of gaps and gaping holes—
for example, those who used their mouth for malice.
A Jew who was ashamed of his own *Yiddishkeit* is
treated there for rheumatoid arthritis.

XLVI

" 'Not me! Not me! It couldn't be,' I pled,
and vehemently I commenced to tremble
as I was dragged toward a vacant bed.
Of course, it was pointless of me to dissemble.
Yet this was only intended as a warning,
and I slept very comfortably till morning.
From there, we visited the Holy Temple—
no, not the Third: the one the Edomites destroyed,
leaving in every Jew an aching void.

XLVII

"They introduced me to a morose fella,
who proved to be none other than Karl Marx.
He showed me around the far end of Machpela—
Hebron's caves—where lie our Patriarchs.
Looking quite stoned, as if he were on drugs,
he pointed out a row of jars and jugs,
containing each a quantity of sparks
kindled by daily Torah study, acts of charity,
and prayers to G–d in purity and sincerity.

XLVIII

"Accounting for each gram of this great treasure,
he shlepps these vessels to the river Dinur,
and empties them according to strict measure,
whence flows the river downward to inciner-
ate the evil and hate which stalk the earth—
and would destroy it for a pennyworth!—
thus kindling hot repentance in a sinner.
Back, then, return those vessels, once they've been decanted,
poised to receive the prayers that G–d has granted.

XLIX

"Thence were we led into another chamber—
the chamber of arts and music and the sciences,
to get to which, we had to crawl and clamber
over obstacles and most unholy alliances.
'Ach! Ganif!' cried Reb Marx in indignation.
'He's tried to pry the lid off Inspiration
again, in spite of all my dire defiances—
and in the process smashed the jug containing Rhyme!
Verzeihen Sie, bitte! He does this all the time!'

L

"By the time we read the portion, 'Get thee out
of thy country, thy folk, thy father's house,'
our trek had brought me, like an eagel scout,
to journey's end. But like a frightened mouse
I stood before the doors of the *Beis Din*—
the rabbinical tribunal. What? Waltz in?
I heard the music, and it wasn't Strauss—
although my circumstance might have inspired Liszt to
compose a waltz—the one they call *Mephisto!*

XLVIII: Ganif (Yid.): thief.
     Verzeihen Sie, bitte (Germ.): Please excuse me!

" ' *Ach! Ganif!'* cried Reb Marx in indignation."

LI

"Indeed, it seems what specially exercized
the Court was what I wrote about Creation
in a book I fear was overpublicized,
as my Accuser said in his relation.
But here is how the Prosecutor put it—
leaving my planned defense completely gutted:
'Professor Gansa, you are by reputation
a man of truth, of honor, of intellect and science,
on whom the public places much reliance:

LII

" 'You wrote a book in which you boldly claim
that science is the one hope for humanity,
comparing science to a flickering flame
that could ameliorate the world's insanity.
We read your book; we comprehend your views
on G–d, on Judaism and the Jews.
The book contains a great deal of inanity.
However, this is not a court of inquisition,
and we respect your right to your position.

LIII

" 'Nevertheless, when the likes of you purport
to prove or to disprove a G–d Creator,
and use your math and method to distort
while waving high your fame and calculator,
that is a matter which we can't ignore.
For this we've summoned you to Judgement's door,
to be tried as scoffer and prevaricator.
Speak truth when called upon, and let the truth suffice:
as Einstein said, "G–d does not play at dice."

LIV

" 'It seems you claim, if infinitely old,
the universe could not have been created!
Indeed, you make so infinitely bold
as to suggest that this is what is stated
by the *Rambam* in his *Guide to the Perplexed*—
a serious misreading of the text!
From there, you argue that an uncreated,
endless universe could not have a Creator—
a thesis fit for the perambulator!

LV

" 'Indeed, this is an ancient paradox.
For every egg implies a prior chicken,
and infinite past is writ on brand-new clocks
and on every living thing that G–d doth quicken.
Because, what G–d creates, He makes from nil,
with nothing but an act of simple will,
from which every material cause is stricken.
What should a universe add on to what is told?
And just because it's infinitely old?

LVI

" 'You have a little grandson—do you not?—
whose favorite occupation is blowing bubbles.
You've watched him blow, enraptured, lost in thought;
what need have you of telescopes and Hubbles?
The tip of a toddler's straw appoints a globe,
swelling and growing, till he withdraws the probe.
Detached, it hangs in the air, shimmers and wobbles,
then floats away, the wind's pearl, seamless and unbounded.
That toddler leaves great theorists confounded!

LIV: "a serious misreading of the text!": See Note 4 at end.

LVI: "That toddler leaves great theorists confounded!": See Note 5 at end.

"That toddler leaves great theorists confounded!"

LVII

" 'Indeed, they'd prove the cosmos always was,
by doubling back upon itself time's swath,
thus to remove the need for a Prime Cause.
For this, they have no need of higher math:
they might as well say of themselves, "Before
I was, was nothing, nothing when I'm no more;
between two nothings stretches my life-path:
therefore the span—my being—is all I place before me.
I have no need of G–d or of her who bore me!"

LVIII

" 'But still, all this is mostly metaphysics,
since none but G–d can make *quidquid ex nilo.*
Let us set sail upon the sea of physics,
and try what wind causes your sail to billow.
Suppose a universe *ad infinitum:*
you have some rocket flares and you ignite 'em;
you lay your head upon a magic pillow,
and you await the light, if need be, till eternity,
to see if space is curved and will return it t'ye.

LIX

" 'By your own thinking, you'd evaporate,
your whole existence balk and be erased:
because the rays of light will propagate,
you say, forever throughout the empty waste.
How shan't an act in time make endless waves,
just as a pebble in infinite pond behaves?
It's obvious your theory is falsely based,
even as you genuflect to logic, overawed—
a blasphemy of physics, your false god!

_____

LVII: quidquid ex nilo (Lat.): something from nothing.

LX

" 'How should we sentence one who has G–d banished
on the ground that He creates something infinite?
Should not the same logic pronounce you vanished,
as one who digs in quicksand must sink in it?
We've said enough. Prepare now to defend
yourself, for by yourself are you condemned.
Can a spider caught in its own web unspin it?
Consider Haman, hanged on gallows he had built.
Had he prevailed, it's your blood he'd have spilt!' "

LXI

"I crumpled when I heard that end of speech.
But as a drowning man clutches at straws,
I seized the only flotsam within reach.
'May it please the Court: my book has many flaws.
But if my punishment is carried out,
my book will only propagate more doubt
and disrepect for Torah and its laws.
Whereas if you let me live a while, I can recant
and free the world from a hefty load of cant.'

LXII

"So, Doctor, as you see, they let me go.
They sent me to a kind of halfway house
up in the hills, where I grew *aricots*
and missed my kids, my campus and my spouse.
It had a laboratory, well-equipped,
and what it lacked was punctually shipped.
I lived there many months without a grouse,
thanks to a library stocked with encyclopedias,
which I read until the alphabet grew tedious.

LX: "it's your blood he'd have spilt!": See Note 6 at end.

LXIII

"In fact, as time progressed, my spirit wilted.
My laboratory work was pure routine.
Above all else, I felt, quite frankly, jilted,
as I heard no more from my old friend -stein (or -steen).
Indeed, I yearned for him with a great yearning,
and missed our daily bouts of Torah learning
as we strolled beneath the hedgerow on the green.
Of course, I walked abroad when weary from the lab,
but now the scenery seemed so very drab.

LXIV

"Where were the forests and far-flung expanses,
the gentle sine wave of the hills and valleys,
the unearthly light that pristinely enhances
the pages of unworldly *Rand-McNalleys?*
Where were the singing trees, the dancing shadows
that fled, at our approach, across the meadows,
the soldier-ranks of rye that the wind rallies,
the high cathedral vaults of overarching branches,
the whipped-cream peaks smoking with avalanches?

LXV

"Alas, those sights were uniformly greyed
by a kind of fog that clung to all outdoors,
so that when I walked, I generally strayed
until I came home crawling on all fours—
like the nights I used to hunt my parking spot
while stumbling round the campus parking lot.
By the time I'd read up to the Persian Wars,
I had devised a grand, ingenious experiment,
for lack of better enterprise or merriment.

LXVI

"For reading the encyclopedia articles,
I came upon one by Professor Hawking,
on quantum physics and atomic particles.
On earth, I wouldn't have known what he was talking
about, but there it all seemed very clear.
I got a blinding flash, and here's the idea:
There is a quark that physicists are stalking—
beyond the quarks known as Top, Bottom, Charm and Strange—
which, mercifully, lies beyond their range—

LXVII

"a mini-black hole, to use an alias,
at the bottom of a well of gravity—
an infinitely concentrated mass,
about ten billion billion GeV.
Till now, the particle investigators
have used big guns—proton accelerators—
against nuclei held in captivity.
Such methods will not work with said mini-black hole,
as it would promptly eat the protons whole!

LXVIII

"The way to do it, Doctor, it occurred to me,
was, shoot a stream of anti-gravitons—
a theory which seemed not at all absurd to me,
as they abound in the upper echelons.
It shouldn't take much juice to pierce the shell
of such a quark and blow it all to hell . . . !
Suppose you split a thin beam of photons:
each photon half acts as a whole—the other's clone!
What if all superquarks were alike as one?

LXVI: Top, Bottom, Charm and Strange: puckish names for puckish
particles, but real, nonetheless.

LXVII: GeV: giga-electron-volt. 1 GeV = 1 billion electron volts.

LXIX

"In short, I guessed that every superquark
was like a window into the Big Bang,
and all you had to do was blow a spark
through one to re-explode the whole shebang!
Without a qualm, without a moral query,
I built an apparatus to test my theory.
I called it 'Gansa's Project Yin & Yang',
fully prepared to make the world a palimpsest!
Oh, how I fell! Oh how I failed that test!

LXX

"How could I, Carlo Gansa, fall so low?
I ask myself that question every day.
There is so much I love down here, below.
I guess up there it seemed so far away.
And yet, that other world is as close to this
as lovers joined in an eternal kiss!
So there you have it. What more is there to say?
I've told you all I can recall—the *gansa Megilla*:
I thought I'm G–d, and ended up Godzilla.

LXXI

"My finger was already on the button,
when I felt a gentle pressure on my hand—
a familiar touch—and woke up of a sudden,
my wife beside me, a rose on the bedstand."
Gansa fell silent. Something like a sigh
escaped his chest. He fiddled with his tie.
He looked a wanderer from an alien land.
How strange the demons that inhabit the hidden hollows
of the human mind! I answered him as follows:

LXX: gansa Megilla: Literally, "the entire scroll", a Yiddish expression
meaning "the whole story".

LXXII

"Listening to your story, esteemed Professor,
I'm struck again by the self-healing power
of the human psyche. For I am not the possessor,
as the 'in' psychiatrist of a transient hour,
of a magic key or patent-pending nostrum
to restore you to your status quo and rostrum.
What I possess is a key to unlock the tower
in which the mind imprisons its own best physician . . ."
(The speech was stock, so skip, with my permission . . .

LXXIII

. . . to where I talk of needing to belong,
and how neglect of our ancestral ties,
and so on and so forth—you know the song.)
"The dream you had impresses me as wise.
You don't need me; just follow its prescription."
Here, Gansa threw a genuine conniption.
"What dream!" he shrieked, and pulled down his Levis,
exposing the ancestral tie sealed in his member.
"That wasn't there," he cried, "before last September!"

LXXIII: That wasn't there . . . before last September: See Note 7 at end.

"...I felt a gentle pressure on my hand..."

LXXIV

But here I draw a veil over the strange case
of Professor Carlo Gansa and what he dreamed.
There's more to it than is printed on its face,
the treatment more complex than first it seemed,
presenting aspects worthy of discussion
in English, German, French, and *Mamaloshon.*
But I'm about to have myself up-beamed,
as none of that is likely to be thought essential.
The poem is done. The rest is confidential!

LXXV

Only this I'd like to add, as I depart
for worlds unknown beyond the furthest reaches
of inner space, where dwells the human heart—
what Science must learn, what Gansa's story teaches:
Love truth, but ever-so-cautiously pursue it:
it pursueth thee! Celebrity? Eschew it.
Question authority, agenda and aegis.
And remember Gansa, who scoured the cosmos for a clue
to what he should have known—and always knew!

Finis

LXXIV: Mamaloshon: literally, "mother tongue", *i.e.,* Yiddish.

"I am a Jew...!"

NOTES

(Comprising a Brief Exposé of Carl Sagan's *Demon-Haunted World: Science as a Candle in the Dark.*)*

1. Sagan devotes not less than 70 pages (the citations are too many to list) to a critical discussion of alleged UFO sightings and "alien abductions". Alleged sexual probing of alleged abductees by alleged aliens is discussed or mentioned at pp. 63-5, 109-10; 124-27, 130, 132, 147, 154-60, 182, 184-86, 188, 191-93, and 198. Sagan compares such reports, without critical discussion—and without an even elementary understanding of these subjects—to stories from Genesis and the Talmud (124) and to the alleged "hoax" of Deuteronomy. (91) Equally unsubstantiated is his rather startling allegation that "the government and munificently funded civic groups systematically distort and even invent scientific evidence of adverse effects" of drugs—"especially marijuana", in an all-out campaign in which "no public official is permitted even to raise the topic for open discussion." (415) Concerning telepathy, Sagan magnanimously concedes: "It is barely possible that a few of these paranormal claims might one day be verified by solid scientific data." (224). However the examples he selects are clearly slanted toward ridicule. (194, 198, 221, 224). About homeopathy, Sagan has nothing more to offer than a snide reference to "water remembering what molecules used to be dissolved in it" (222)—an attitude that reminds one of the scornful hostility once reserved by western medicine for Chinese acupuncture. Sagan's discussion of the legendary "canals" on Mars (48-49) is prelude to a needlessly prolonged examination of alleged "faces" on the Martian surface. Sagan devotes at least twelve pages (118-23; 406-413) to a condensed and graphic history of the persecution of "witches", culminating in the following abject outburst: "The witch mania is shameful. How could we do it? How could we be so ignorant about ourselves and our weaknesses?" (413) *We??* In a book billed as a manifesto against ignorance, bigotry and inhumanity, in which are to be found perhaps two or three oblique references to the Holocaust and not one word about the Marranos, such self-incrimination, by a virtual member of that other class of victims of the Inquisition, is, to say the

---

* Citations to *The Demon-Haunted World* refer to the Ballantine paperback edition (1997).

least, puzzling. For under duress of the terrible persecutions of 1391 and 1412, a large portion of Spanish Jewry converted to Christianity, only to be terrorized, tortured and burnt as "Marranos" ("swine") upon the same racks and pyres on which were, or would be, immolated Sagan's "witches". *How could we do it!*

In regard to necromancy, or "channelling", as he calls it, Sagan is more restrained. He doesn't "guffaw at the woman who visits her husband's grave and chats him up every now and then." He is only leery of "a practice rife with fraud". Here, in contrast to his handling of other dubious topics, his treatment of the subject is brief, to the point, and of considerable interest. The best part of Sagan's book is the case he makes for education as the foundation of freedom and democracy. Regrettably, however, he is principally concerned with science education, while the relevance of the humanities seems largely to have passed him by. Indeed, Sagan himself evinces scant familiarity with the methodological foundations of humanistic research, and repeatedly commits the same kind of mistake that he criticizes in exponents of the pseudosciences. Note for example, his flatly erroneous assertion, " '[D]emon' *means* 'knowledge' in Greek"— which absurdity is amplified by the following nonsensical footnote: " 'Science means 'knowledge' in Latin. A jursidictional dispute is exposed, even if we look no further." (116) Additional examples abound below.

2. Sagan's treatment of Judaism and the Jews is obscured, to some degree, by his lumping them together with other religions he considers "fundamentalist", and, on the other hand, by his generally contemptuous attitude towards the Bible (particularly the Old Testament), and still further by his rather patronizing attempt to distinguish "Mainstream" Judaism from Orthodoxy and Conservativism—a distinction which, besides being inaccurate (few would argue with Conservative Judaism's claim to mainstreamism!), cannot be totally sincere, since even Reform Judaism strongly endorses the ritual of circumcision, which Sagan pointedly ridicules! (275)

The very application of the word "fundamentalist" to Orthodox Judaism is highly offensive. Webster's authoritative Second Edition (1934) defines "fundamentalism" as "[a] recent movement in American Protestantism in opposition to modernistic tendencies, re-emphasizing as fundamental to Christianity the inerrancy of the Scriptures, Biblical miracles . . . and substitutional atonement." Since Judaism depends on the Oral Law for its understanding of Scripture, from whose apparent literal meaning it frequently differs, and whose actual meaning it constantly questions, and since it has never responded to the relatively recent Reform and Conservative movements with a movement of reaction, the application of "fundamentalist" to Judaism is both inept and misleading. The ineptness is heightened when one considers the more recent association of the term "fundamentalist" with various militant groups within Islam which have espoused terror and "Jihad" as means to both political ends and spiritual salvation—the political ends being, at the very least, the destruction of the Jewish State (although how this could occur without the destruction of Jews has never been—nor need it be—explained). Thus, on p. 222, Sagan refers to "fundamentalist Christians and Jews", while, on p. 277, obviously ignorant of the Talmudic method so basic to Orthodox Jewish teaching and practice, he writes that while

> "[s]ome of mainstream Christianity and Judaism embraces ...at least a portion of the humility, self-criticism, reasoned debate, and questioning of received wisdom that the best of science offers . . . *other sects* (italics added), sometimes called conservative or fundamentalist . . . have chosen to make a stand on matters subject to disproof, and thus have something to fear from science."

In this respect, it is notable that while conceding that "fundamentalist Christians and Jews" have rejected many of the superstitions so repugnant to him "because the Bible so enjoins", he still finds it hard to forgive the "author of Deuteronomy" for not arguing "that such practices fail to deliver what they promise", while instead condemning them as " 'abominations'—perhaps suitable for other nations, but not for the followers of G–d"! Whereas, he adds with a lusty twist of the knife, "even the Apostle Paul, so credulous on so many matters, counsels us to 'prove all things.' " (222-23)

The credulity of the Jews is evidently a matter of special weight to Sagan, as he troubles himself, in his brief dissertation on demons, to note that "Maimonides denied their reality, but the overwhelming majority of rabbis believed in *dybbuks*." (118) Now, a dybbuk is certainly not a demon, and its reality, as a psychological phenomenon, is medically attested, though perhaps not yet well understood. See *Encyclopedia Judaica, vol 6,* at *Dibbuk:* "The phenomena connected with the beliefs in and the stories about *dibbukim* usually have their factual background in cases of hysteria and sometimes even in manifestations of schizophrenia." Naturally, Sagan cites no source for his conclusions regarding the majority beliefs of rabbis. Indeed, Sagan makes it pretty clear that, for him, the authenticity (let alone veracity!) of Judaism itself is not deserving of serious discussion. "A more or less typical example [of a politically motivated hoax] is the book of Deuteronomy—discovered hidden in the Temple in Jerusalem by King Josiah, who, miraculously, in the midst of a major reformation

struggle, found in Deuteronomy confirmation of all his views." (91)
As every educated Jew knows, this mindlessly repeated canard was
the brainchild of Julius Wellhausen (originator of the so-called "higher
Biblical criticism" and a reputed Jew-hater) and is entirely based on
Wellhausen's mistranslation of the term *Sefer haTorah* (meaning a
complete scroll of the Pentateuch) as "a Book (*i.e., one* of the five
books) of the Torah"!

Most shocking of all is Sagan's underhanded imputation of cruelty
to the Jewish Religion and People. In a section purporting to unmask
the rhetorical devices by which "baloney" artists commonly evade
criticism, Sagan poses the following question:

> "How could G[-]d permit the followers of Judaism,
> Christianity, and Islam—each in their own way enjoined to
> heroic measures of loving kindness and compassion—to have
> perpetrated so much cruelty for so long?" (213)

Sagan answers this specious conundrum with an example of what he
terms the "special plead" (as if to imply that the question is
unanswerable without resorting to further "baloney"):

> "You don't understand Free Will again, and anyway, G[-]d moves
> in mysterious ways." (213)

Thus, the special and perennial victims of the horrendous persecutions
of Christians and Muslims are equated—cynically, and quite
baldly—with their persecutors! Predictably, Sagan fails to ground this
vile smear upon anything he himself would consider reliable evidence.
To justify it, he must reach far back into a document for which he
nurtures an unwavering and jaundiced distrust:

> "In Joshua and in the second half of Numbers is celebrated
> [sic!] the mass murder of men, women, children, down to the
> domestic animals in city after city across the whole land of
> Canaan . . . The only justification offered for this slaughter is
> the mass murderers' claim that, in exchange for circumcising
> their sons and adopting a particular set of rituals, their
> ancestors were long before promised that this land was their
> land.... And these events are not incidental, but central to the
> main narrative thrust of the Old Testament. Similar stories of
> mass murder (and in the case of the Amalekites, genocide) can
> be found in the books of Saul [sic!], Esther, and elsewhere in
> the Bible, with hardly a pang of moral doubt." (290)

That such statements are nothing less than the usual blood libel (not far removed from its grand prototype of Jesus being murdered by the Jews!) is perhaps disguised by the disingenuous attempt to take its proof from the Jews' own holy texts. It is curious to note how often those same secularists who uncritically disparage the veracity of the Jewish Bible will unhesitatingly mine those same texts for historical dirt to throw at the Jews and the Jewish heritage! One should be entitled to ask why, alone among the nations of the earth, who have enthusiastically subjected one another, since the appearance of homo erectus, to mutual atrocity, the Jews have been honored here with the horrific distinction of "mass murderers". The boastful stele of Egyptian Pharoah Merneptah (12th Century B.C.E.) alerts one sufficiently well to the charitable nature of Bible-era warfare as practised by Israel's loving friends and admirers: "Israel is laid waste, his seed is not." *See* J.B. Pritchard, *The Ancient Near East: an Anthology of Texts and Pictures,* Princeton U. Press (1958), p. 231. Ditto, the 9th-Century B.C.E. Moabite Stone, containing the inscription of Mesha, King of Moab:

"And the king of Israel had built Ataroth for [the men of Gad], but I fought against the town and took it and slew all the people of the town as satiation for [the god] Chemosh and Moab. [. . .] And Chemosh said to me, 'Go take Nebo from Israel!' So I went by night and fought against it from the break of dawn until noon, taking it and slaying all, seven thousand men, boys, women, girls and maid-servants, for I had devoted them to destruction for (the god) Ashtar-Chemosh." *Op. cit.,* p. 210.

On the contrary, it can be shown from the Biblical account (which is so far from the "celebration" Sagan would see in it, as to be unique among the coeval chronicles of nations for its forthrightness in recording both triumph and defeat, success and failure, glory and shame!) that the Children of Israel destroyed such of their enemies as it behooved them in order to survive as a nation of law and faith, and that whenever it seemed that the continuity of those things had been secured, they sought coexistence and peace. Moreover, Sagan grossly misrepresents what he calls "the only justification offered for this slaughter": for it is not the Covenant of Abraham alone, as Sagan would have us believe, but the forfeiture of the Land through the abominations of its former inhabitants, as attested by both Biblical testimony and archeological findings. See, for example, Deut. IX, 4-6; XII, 31; XVIII, 9; XXIII, 18-19 (the prohibited *"q'deysha"* in this last passage alludes to the temple prostitutes—*"qudshu"* in Ugaritic—male and female, institutionalized by the Canaanite religion). See also, W.F. Albright, *Archaeology & the Religion of Israel,* (Baltimore, Johns Hopkins Press) 1968, p. 75: "Sacred prostitution was apparently an almost invariable concomitant of the cult of the Phoenician [*i.e.,* Canaanite] and Syrian goddess . . . as we know from many allusions in classical literature, especially in Herodotus, Strabo and Lucian." See also, *op. cit.,* pp. 92-93: "That [human sacrifice] was prevalent [in Phoenicia] in the early first millennium is certain from numerous biblical allusions, as well as from the fact, attested by many Roman witnesses, that the Carthaginians, who migrated from Phoenicia in the ninth and eighth centuries B.C., practiced human sacrifice on a large scale down to the fall of Carthage."

If the measures adopted by the Israelites seem harsh by today's standards (what standards?), they were no less severe when employed by the Israelites against themselves, as can be seen from the war of Gibeah, in which a notorious crime left unpunished by the Benjaminites led to their near extinction. Jud. 19-20. To such observations may be added that if, before the Throne of G–d, the Israelites should indeed be found wanting in mercy, their descendants have already paid the price for it a thousand times over in kind. To ignore this fact, as one must to brand the Jewish People with the crime of "mass murder", one must possess a warped historical and moral judgement indeed.

Sagan's jibes decrease in specificity as they increase in viciousness: "The [cultures, ethnicities and societies] with a supreme god who lives in the sky tend to be the most ferocious—torturing their enemies for example. But this is a statistical correlation only; the causal link has not been established, although speculations naturally present themselves." (296-97) We need only suppress a gasp in order to hear the muffled but hearty guffaws issuing from the tombs of those pluripolytheistic, idol-worshipping masters and devotees of torture—a pale memento of which still hangs in every church and Christian home—the Romans, who elevated the practice into an art, a public spectacle and a mass divertimento!

3. Amalek attacked the Israelites without provocation and from the rear, when the latter were weak from thirst and still in disarray from their escape from Egypt. Exodus XVII, 8-14 and Deuteronomy XXV, 17-19 leave little doubt that the Amalekites sought, and perennially sought, to destroy the Jewish People. What the Bible leaves unsaid there is explicit in the oral tradition preserved in Midrashim and commentators. As for Haman (a descendant of Agag, the Amalekite king spared by Saul's characteristically Jewish compassion!), his genocidal machinations against the Jews are clearly spelled out in the Book of Esther.

4. *A serious misreading of the text:*

> "Moses Maimonides, in his Guide to the Perplexed, held that
> G–d could be truly known only if there were free and open
> study of both physics and theology [I,55] [the citation's are
> Sagan's]. What would happen if science demonstrated an
> infinitely old universe? Then theology would have to be
> seriously revamped [II,25]. Indeed, this is the one conceivable
> finding of science that could disprove a Creator—because an
> infinitely old universe would never have been created. It
> would have always been here." *Sagan,* at p. 278.

What Maimonides actually says, however, is hardly enough to fulfil
Sagan's agenda. In the first place, the point that Maimonides wants to
get across in I,55 is that "nothing can be predicated of G–d that
implies . . . corporeality, emotion or change, non-existence, or
similarity with any of His creatures . . . ." Insofar as we need to
understand the foregoing, "our knowledge of G–d is aided by the
study of Natural Science." *Guide of the Perplexed* (3 volumes in one),
translated and edited by M. Friedländer, Hebrew Publishing Co. (New
York, undated), p. 200. Generally speaking, Maimonides holds, in
accordance with the Aristotelean method, that the study of physics is
ancillary to the study of metaphysics ("the science of G–d"), and
therefore prerequisite to an understanding of the logic, terminology
and metaphors employed by the latter discipline (metaphysics means,
literally, *after the natural sciences*). *Guide,* I, *Introduction,* at pp. 11-
12. Maimonides does *not* hold, as Sagan rashly asserts (278), that a
knowledge of G–d can be achieved by penetrating the mysteries of the
physical universe! And he certainly does *not* hold that the study of
either physics or theology should be "free and open" (*ibid.*). On the
contrary,

> "'[theology] must not be fully expounded even in the presence
> of a single student, unless he be wise and able to reason for
> himself, and even then you should merely acquaint him with
> the heads of the different sections of the subject.' (*Chagigah,
> fol.* 11b)." I, p.8.

Furthermore, "[e]ven with regard to Natural Science, it should be
observed that there are some principles which are not to be explained
in extenso." *Ibid.* Here, at the place cited by Sagan, Maimonides says
that the study of physics can help us acquire an understanding of *four
specified attributes,* and hence learn how they are to be distinguished
from the true attributes of G–d, which, as Maimonides states in I,58,
are all *negative* attributes. (*Note* that Maimonides, logically, considers

44

non-existence as a *positive* attribute of something that cannot be said to exist, rather than as a negative attribute of something that does in fact exist). Clearly, Sagan has misrepresented Maimonides' meaning, both in general and in the cited place. It is precisely to protect Truth from this type of abuse that Maimonides restricts the study of theology, and of some aspects of natural science, to those select few who are intellectually equipped to handle such material!

The second part of Sagan's lecture on Maimonides is, if possible, even more obfuscatory. What Maimonides says in II,25 is that he rejects the eternity of the universe—not because Scripture denies it, but *because it has not been proven:*

> "As there is no proof sufficient to convince us, this theory [Plato's version] need not be taken into consideration, nor the other one [Aristotle's version]; we take the text of the Bible literally, and say that it teaches us a truth which we cannot prove, and that the miracles are evidence for the correctness of our view."

According to Maimonides, Plato's theory posits a primordial substance, coeternal with G–d, but caused by Him, and subject to His will: "G–d can do with it what He pleases: at one time He forms of it heaven and earth, at another time He forms some other thing." II, 13, p. 65. Aristotle's theory—still in the words of Maimonides—posits a universe subject to unchangeable laws:

> "[T]he heavens, which form the permanent element in the universe, and are not subject to genesis and destruction, have always been so; time and motion are eternal, permanent, and have neither beginning nor end." II, 14, p. 66.

It is only if Aristotles' theory were proven that "the whole teaching of Scripture would be rejected, and we should be forced to other opinions." II, 25, at p. 120 Yet, as Maimonides points out, *not even Aristotle rejects the existence of G–d!* "[Aristotle] further says "that G–d produced this universe in its totality by His will, but not from nothing." II, 14, p. 66. See also, *e.g.*, Aristotle, *Metaphysica*, XII, 6-7 (1072a-1075b); *Physica*, VIII, 1 (252b), 10 (267b); *De Caelo* I, 3 (270ab).

Thus, when Maimonides says that if Aristotle is correct, the whole teaching of Scripture would have to be rejected, he cannot mean the existence of G–d, or His creation of the universe, but only the *manner* or *type* of creation! Maimonides hastens to emphasize that such a task would not at all be arduous:

"We should perhaps have had an easier task in showing that the scriptural passages referred to are in harmony with the theory of the Eternity of the Universe . . . than we had in explaining the anthropomorphisms in the Bible when we rejected the idea that G–d is corporeal." II, 25, at p. 118.

Hence, Sagan's assertion that the finding of an infinitely old universe would disprove a Creator is contradicted by the very text Sagan has chosen to dignify his thesis! Sagan's attempt to argue his own case from Maimonides' words is either dishonest or incompetent. *It is a measure of Sagan's integrity as a scholar that he attempts here to pervert the clear words of Maimonides—universally considered one of the principal pillars of modern, Orthodox Judaism—into an argument against the existence of G–d!*

It is also worth noting, in that connection, that Sagan's editors appear to have omitted from the subject index of a book laden with anti-Jewish and anti-religious snipes and barbs, all reference to Judaism, Jewish, Jews, Hebrews, Israelites, Esther, Saul, Talmud, the Bible, the Covenant, or circumcision, as well as anything related to Christianity or Islam—making it discouragingly difficult for any critic to locate the controversial passages in which those words are mentioned. Given this background, one may legitimately wonder why Deuteronomy is listed. Was it left in in order to deflect the inference that is drawn here? Or was it simply that the first time the word occurs, the context is non-controversial; and having cited it once, the editors thought it too obvious to omit the second citation, in which Sagan baldly claims that that Book is a patent hoax?

It must also be said, for the benefit of readers lost in the fog of Sagan's anti-G–d rhetoric, that, as far as proving the eternity of the universe is concerned, Sagan never comes close to delivering the goods! Compare Sagan's introduction to Stephen Hawking's *Brief History of Time:*

"Hawking is attempting . . . to understand the mind of G–d. And this makes all the more unexpected the conclusion of the effort, at least so far: a universe with no edge in space, no beginning or end in time, and nothing for a Creator to do." S.W. Hawking, *A Brief History of Time: From the Big Bang to Black Holes,* Bantam Books (Toronto, New York), 1988, p. x.

However, despite the observed consistency between certain mathematical predictions of the "no boundary condition" and actual measurements of the microwave background radiation, Hawking himself advances nothing resembling a "conclusion":

"The idea that space and time *may* [italics added] form a closed surface without a boundary also has profound implications for the role of G–d in the affairs of the universe." *Hawking*, at p. 140.

It is true that Hawking then asks:

"[I]f the universe is really completely self-contained, having no boundary or edge, it would have neither beginning nor end: it would simply be. What place then for a creator?" *Hawking*, at pp. 140-41.

However, Hawking himself admits that such questions are

"an example of the fallacy, pointed out by St. Augustine, of imagining G–d as a being existing in time: time is a property only of the universe that G–d created. Presumably, [H]e knew what [H]e intended when [H]e set it up!" *Hawking*, at p. 166.

This concept has been fundamental to modern cosmology since at least the publication (1930) of Sir James Jeans's classic, *The Mysterious Universe* (New York, E.P. Dutton & Co., 1958), in which we read the following memorable passage from the concluding chapter (p. 177):

"If the universe is a universe of thought, then its creation must have been an act of thought. Indeed the finiteness of time and space almost compel us, of themselves, to picture the creation as an act of thought; the determination of the constants such as the radius of the universe and the number of electrons it contained imply thought, whose richness is measured by the immensity of these quantities. Time and space, which form the setting for the thought, must have come into being as part of this act. Primitive cosmologies pictured a creator working in space and time, forging sun, moon and stars out of already existent raw material. Modern scientific theory compels us to think of the [C]reator as working outside time and space, which are part of [H]is creation, just as the artist is outside his canvas. It accords with the conjecture of Augustine: 'Non in tempore, sed cum tempore, finxit Deus mundum.'"

It is a curious fact that Jeans's cosmology, still in print seventy years after its appearance, and still quoted in the scientific and philosophical literature, is nowhere cited in either *The Demon-Haunted World,* or in *Cosmos*—not even among the author's suggestions for further reading. Why not? Perhaps because, as Sagan writes in the very first sentence of his *Cosmos* (another pop treatise with an ulterior agenda and an exaggerated reputation), "The Cosmos is all that is or ever was or ever will be"; and, for all his professed belief in "the free exchange of ideas" and "vigorous debate" (*Demon-Haunted World*, p. 38), Sagan is not one to hand out free ammunition to those who might shoot it back.

5. *"That toddler leaves great theorists confounded."* See Sir James Jeans, *The Mysterious Universe*, pp. 135-36:

> "To sum up, a soap-bubble with irregularities and corrugations on its surface is perhaps the best representation, in terms of simple and familiar materials, of the new universe revealed to us by the theory of relativity. The universe is not the interior of the soap-bubble but its surface, and we must always remember that, while the surface of the soap-bubble has only two dimensions, the universe-bubble has four—three dimensions of space and one of time. And the substance out of which this bubble is blown, the soap-film, is empty space welded on to empty time."

Just as it is impossible, by examining the bubble itself, to determine how—*or if*—it was created, so it is impossible, without extra-universal data, to resolve conclusively the problem of the origin of the universe. And yet, argues the toddler, *Someone* created it, as I have created this bubble!

6. *"It's your blood he'd have spilt!"* At the time of Haman's plot to annihilate the Jewish subjects of the Persian Empire, substantially all Jews who had survived the Babylonian conquest were living under Persian rule. Thus, if Haman had succeeded, he would have wiped out the Jewish People, including, in all probability, Gansa's own ancestors.

7. The pre-abduction condition of Gansa's member is derived from what is perhaps the most offensive passage in Sagan's book:

> "Does the occasional uncircumcised Jewish man fare worse than his co-religionists who abide by the ancient covenant in which G–d demands a piece of foreskin from every male worshiper?" (275)

Not only does Sagan ridicule the covenantal, or religious, aspect of the ritual, but he misrepresents its intended focus and purpose. The focus is every son of a Jewish mother, not "every male worshiper", and the primary purpose is the foundation of his Jewish identity, not the procurement of some hypothetical advantage! Sagan is obviously unaware of the thousands of Jewish emigrés who have been thronging to the *Mohalim*—rabbis trained in the surgical procedure and complex ritual laws of circumcision—ever since the first lifting of the barriers against Jewish emigration from the now defunct Soviet Union. No, those Jews did not fare well under the Soviets! Indeed, circumcision, along with all other traditional Jewish observances, was outlawed and punishable by execution, imprisonment, or exile to Siberia, under an oppressive regime whose anti-religious views had much in common with Sagan's. But putting aside the special question of Soviet Jewry, circumcision is considered by Jews to be so fundamental to Jewish identity, that the practice is pretty much universally accepted, irrespective of the actual beliefs of the parents. In other words, the vast majority of Jewish parents consider it beneficial for their children simply to be endowed with a clear and strong Jewish identity—the obvious exception being those parents who are ashamed of it themselves or view it as something to be suppressed. Surely, any other hypothetical benefit to the child is supremely secondary in this context! In fact, the question posed here by Sagan is so bizarre as to suggest a highly personal animus, not inconsistent with the conjectural interpretation I have put on it. For had Sagan merely intended to raise the age-old question of whether circumcision is medically justifiable, he would not have had to limit his comparison to Jews! Here, however, we are in no need of subtleties: by raising the age-old spectre of Shylock against the Jews, the Jewish G–d, and the Jewish religion, Sagan has painted himself clear enough for anyone who has the courage to look.

ABOUT THE AUTHOR

Born and bred in a Los Angeles briar patch, Peter Gimpel acquired his educational tar and feathers in the august city of Perugia, Italy, where he lived, loved, labored and learned for about one fifth of his current years. Besides *Gansa,* his writings include *The Carnevalis of Eusebius Asch* (a novel), and *Twilight with Halfmoon Rising,* (a selection of his poems). Both works have won high critical praise, *The Carnevalis* being one of the few novels ever to have been reviewed by a journal of philosophy. Peter Gimpel is also the author of a controversial monograph on the Proem of Lucretius, in which the Roman philosopher-poet's daunting Introduction to the *De Rerum Natura*—his great treatise *On Nature*—is plausibly restored to its original sequential order and rhetorical brilliance.

ABOUT THE ILLUSTRATOR

Gerry McGuinness has been a cartoonist since his pudgy little fingers could hold a crayon. Author of the popular political comic strip *Quack and Quail,* Gerry's cartoons and strips have appeared in numerous books, newspapers and magazines, and even on television. A Dubliner by birth, Gerry has an uncannily intuitive grasp of Jewish matters. Gerry's drawings for the present volume are much more than illustrations. They are a Rod-Serlingesque adventure in transpersonal visualization—a phenomenon not unworthy of Professor Gansa's dream.

ABOUT RED HEIFER PRESS

Red Heifer Press is a small, independent press devoted to the publishing and audiopublishing of works of unusual interest and merit in literary fiction, poetry, documentary memoirs, belles lettres, Torah/Judaica, sheet music, and scholarship in the Humanities. For further information about Red Heifer Press, or to view our growing catalog of fine books and compact discs, please visit our website at www.redheiferpress.com.

Readers' comments are welcome and should be directed to:
editor@redheiferpress.com

THIS BOOK WAS PRINTED AND BOUND BY

Sheridan Books, Inc.
100 North Staebler Road
Ann Arbor, Michigan 48103